Night Shadows

BARBARA DaCOSTA

ILLUSTRATED BY **ED YOUNG**

SEVEN STORIES PRESS

New York · Oakland · Liverpool

Night shadows fell on Mrs. Lucy's garage wall.

"Come on," a voice whispered. "Gimme the spray paint."

"Here."

Pfft! Bold, swirling letters appeared.

Suddenly, a door banged open.

"Who's out there?" Mrs. Lucy's sharp voice cut through the night air.

"Run!" Footsteps pounded down the alley.

The next morning, as the sun shone on the waking-up alley, Mrs. Lucy studied the damage to her garage wall.

"Good morning," called out Mr. Jackson, putting his trash in the bin. "Too bad, you've got graffiti again."

"It's those boys," Mrs. Lucy grumbled, fetching her painting supplies.

Nearby, the neighbor boys gathered.
"C'mon, guys, let's play ball!"
They began choosing sides.

"Go on, get out of here," Mrs. Lucy scolded them. "Go play somewhere else."

She climbed up on her step stool and started covering the graffiti, her paint roller going *squish-squeak, squish-squeak.*

The boys sauntered off, and set up a bit further down the alley. Young Tasha came trailing after them, wanting to play.

"Go on, Tasha! Get out of the way!" the boys yelled.

Tasha frowned. "They never let me play," she glumly kicked at pebbles as she wandered back up the alley.
When she got to Mrs. Lucy's garage, she stopped and watched.

"What are you doing?" she asked.

"Covering up this mess," said Mrs. Lucy.

"Can I help?"

Mrs. Lucy glanced down at Tasha. "I suppose so.
You could get those patches down there where
I can't reach."

Tasha took the roller. Squatting,
she painted up-and-down and
sideways, *squish-squeak,*
squish-squeak.

When they were done, Tasha
followed Mrs. Lucy inside
to clean up, and to have
some milk and cookies.

That night, though, it happened again.
Figures crept through the dark.
"Go on, I dare you!" snickered one voice.
Pfft! Broad, circling words formed.

Suddenly, a window opened.
"You boys ought to be ashamed of yourselves!"
   Mrs. Lucy's angry words echoed down the dark alley.
"Run!" The shadowy figures fled into the night.

The next morning, Mrs. Lucy stood looking at the
   marred wall, shaking her head.
She sighed and got out her painting supplies again.
Soon, Tasha showed up.
"See what those boys did?" Mrs. Lucy said, pointing at
   the marks.
"Can I help?" asked Tasha.
Without a word, Mrs. Lucy handed her the paint roller.
Tasha reached and rolled, *squish-squeak, squish-squeak*.
When they were done, they went in to clean up and
   have a snack.

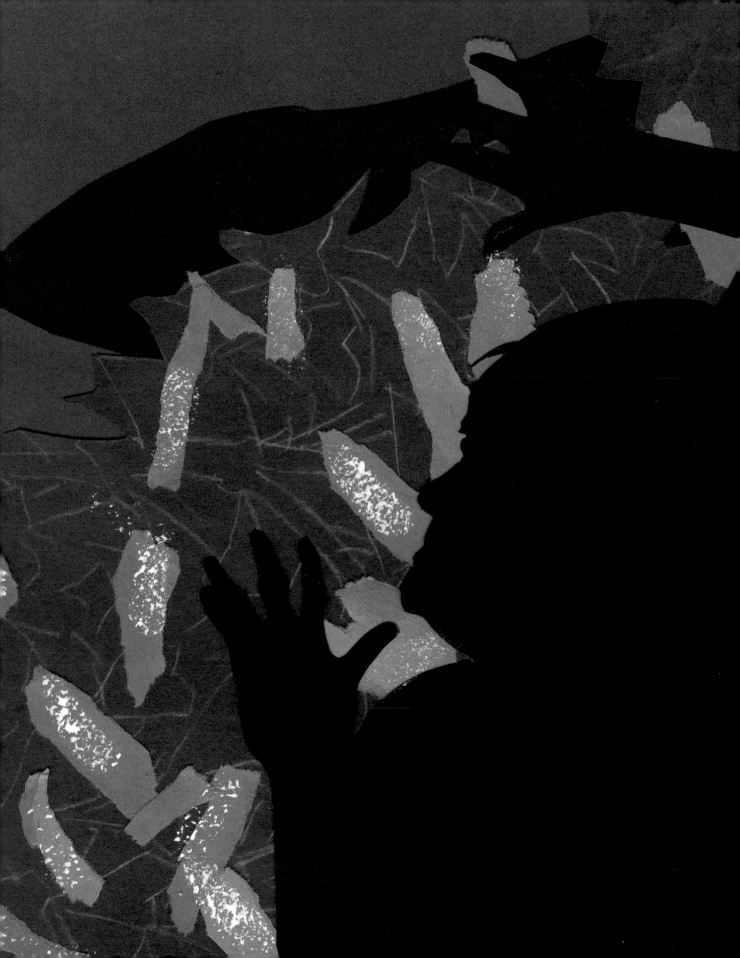

That night, Mrs. Lucy said to herself, "I'm not going to stand for this any longer." She hid behind the lilac bushes by the garage and waited.

Soon came the soft, careful tread of tennis shoes sneaking down the dark alley. A solitary figure this time, face hidden by a sweatshirt hood. The vandal took out a can of paint.

Pfft! Stumbling strokes began to take shape, when suddenly—

"I'll get you—" Mrs. Lucy jumped
out and grabbed the hooded figure. "I'm going to call the police—"
"Stop, Mrs. Lucy. Stop!"
"Tasha?"
Mrs. Lucy pulled down Tasha's
hood to look her in the face.
"Tasha, what's going on? How
could you?"
"I just—I just wanted to come over
again," Tasha cried softly.

Mrs. Lucy didn't know what to say. She stood there for a moment, then reached out her hand.

"Come on, Tasha," she said. "Time to get you home. We've got a lot of work to do tomorrow."

"Together?" asked Tasha.

"Together," said Mrs. Lucy.

One never knows
if there's a tomorrrow.
Today is real.
Take care of yourself
and extend that care
to those around you.
—ED YOUNG

❧ ❧

To Mary Lucy and all those wonderful people
who take time to extend a helping hand.
—BARBARA DaCOSTA

❧ ❧

This learned I from the shadow of a tree,
That to and fro did sway upon a wall, —
Our shadow-selves, our influence, may fall
Where we can never be.
—ANNA E. HAMILTON (1843–1875)

A TRIANGLE SQUARE BOOK FOR YOUNG READERS

published by
SEVEN STORIES PRESS

First Triangle Square edition January 2021

SEVEN STORIES PRESS
140 Watts Street
New York, NY 10013

LIBRARY OF CONGRESS CATALOGING-IN-PUBLICATION DATA

Names: DaCosta, Barbara, author.
Young, Ed, illustrator.
Title: Night Shadows / Barbara DaCosta; illustrated by Ed Young.
Description: New York : Seven Stories Press, 2020.
Audience: Ages 5-8.
Summary: Mrs. Lucy finds graffiti painted on her garage two nights
in a row, but as Tasha, a lonely neighbor girl, helps her paint over it the
two become friends, despite their age difference. Features cut-out illustrations.
Identifiers: LCCN 2020040756 (print) | LCCN 2020040757 (ebook) | ISBN
9781644210246 (hardcover) | ISBN 9781644210253 (epub)
Subjects: CYAC: Graffiti—Fiction. | Friendship—Fiction. |
Neighborhoods—Fiction.
Classification: LCC PZ7.D1218 Nid 2020 (print) | LCC PZ7.D1218 (ebook) |
DDC [E]—dc23
LC record available at https://lccn.loc.gov/2020040756
LC ebook record available at https://lccn.loc.gov/2020040757

College professors and high school and middle school teachers may
order free examination copies of Seven Stories Press titles.
To order, visit www.sevenstories.com or send
a fax on school letterhead to (212) 226-1411.

DESIGN BY Ed Young & Stewart Cauley
WITH EDITORIAL AND DESIGN HELP FROM Shayan Saalabi & Elisa Taber

2 4 6 8 9 7 5 3 1

Printed in China